For Quentin and Katrina.
In memory of Plato. —J.H.

To Fred Frumberg and the brave and excellent
Cambodian dancers of Amrita Performing Arts
—P.L.

Text copyright © 2013 by Joan Heilbroner
Cover art and interior illustrations copyright © 2013 by Pascal Lemaitre

Visit us on the Web!
randomhouse.com/kids

Educators and librarians, for a variety of teaching tools, visit us at RHTeachersLibrarians.com

Library of Congress Cataloging-in-Publication Data
Heilbroner, Joan.
A pet named Sneaker / by Joan Heilbroner ; illustrated by Pascal Lemaitre. — 1st ed.
  p. cm. — (Beginner books)
Summary: Sneaker the snake is not only a good pet for Pete, he becomes a good student at Pete's
school and a hero at the public swimming pool.
ISBN 978-0-307-97580-5 (trade) — ISBN 978-0-375-97116-7 (lib. bdg) —
ISBN 978-0-375-98112-8 (ebook)
[1. Snakes as pets—Fiction.] I. Lemaitre, Pascal, ill. II. Title.
PZ7.H366Pet 2013 [E]—dc23 2011047340

Printed in the United States of America

10 9 8 7 6 5 4 3 2 1

First Edition

A Pet Named Sneaker

By Joan Heilbroner
Illustrated by Pascal Lemaitre

BEGINNER BOOKS®

A Division of Random House, Inc.

There once was a snake
named Sneaker.
He lived in a pet store.
It was a nice store.
But Sneaker was not happy.
He wanted a home.

Many people came into the store.

They took home fish.

They took home birds.

They took home hamsters.

But they did not take home Sneaker.
No one wanted a snake.

Then one day,

a boy came into the store.

His name was Pete.

Pete liked Sneaker.
Sneaker could do
funny things.
"Will you come home
with me?" asked Pete.
Sneaker said,
"Yesssssssssssssssssss!"
He had a home at last!

Sneaker liked his new home.

He had fun with Pete.

He played

I Am a Necktie,

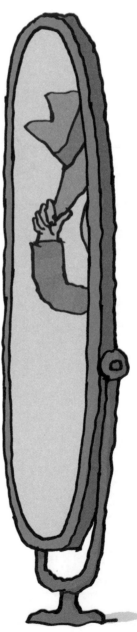

I Am a Hat,

and I Am Handcuffs.

The next morning, Pete said,
"Goodbye, Sneaker.
I have to go to school today."

But Sneaker did not
want to be alone.
So he snuck into
Pete's backpack.

Pete took his backpack to school.
He hung it on his chair.
Sneaker was watching the children.
They were having show-and-tell.

Then Pete saw Sneaker.

He picked him up

and showed him to the class.

"This is my pet snake," he said.

"His name is Sneaker."

"Eww . . . snakes are slimy!" said one kid.

"Snakes are gross," said another.

Then a brave girl
picked up Sneaker.
He was not slimy.
He felt quite nice.

Soon everyone wanted
to play with Sneaker.

Sneaker liked school.

He went back every day.

One day, the teacher drew a picture.

She put letters under it—

a *C,* an *A,* and a *T.*

"What does that spell?"
asked the teacher.
Everyone said, "Cat!"

Sneaker could not say *cat*.

But he could spell *cat*.

And soon he could spell more words.

Rat and *pat*

and *pet* and *net*

and *set* and *seat*.

And then one day, he spelled . . .

"Good work!" said the teacher.
Sneaker was very proud!

The next day, Sneaker
did not go to school.
He went to the park with Pete.

It was summer now.

They went to a nice, cool pool.

Pete jumped into the pool.

He kicked and splashed and swam.

Sneaker wanted to jump in, too.

But Sneaker saw a sign.

And he could read it!

The sign said, "NO PETS."

Sneaker slid behind a rock.

He looked back at the pool.

He saw a little boy

playing with a ball.

Then the ball rolled
into the pool.
And the boy went in
after it.

But the boy did not kick
or splash or swim.
And he did not
come out of
the pool!

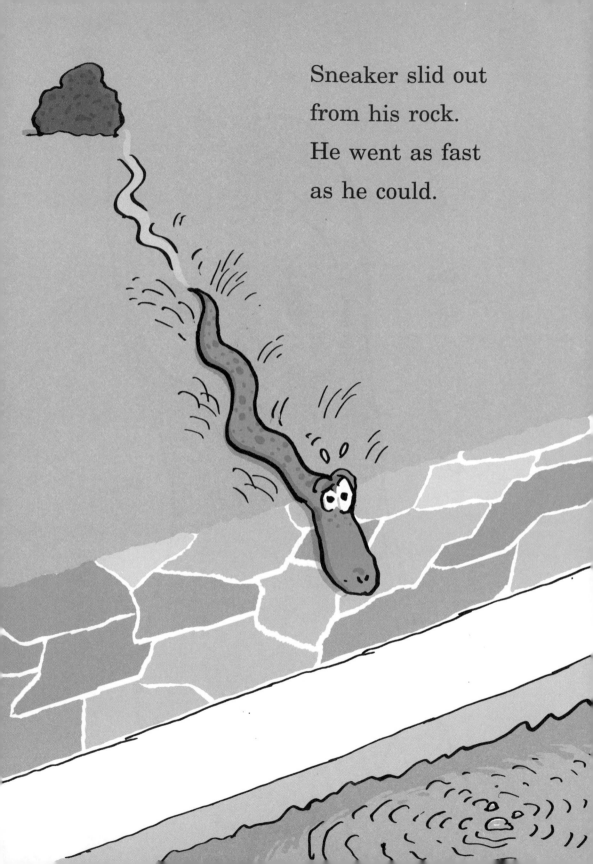

Sneaker slid out
from his rock.
He went as fast
as he could.

Sneaker slid into the pool.

He swam until he came to the boy.

Then Sneaker wrapped himself
around the boy . . .

. . . swam to the top . . .

. . . and pulled him
out of the water.

Sneaker had saved the little boy!

"Hooray for Sneaker!" everyone cheered.
"He is a very brave snake."

The lifeguard smiled at Sneaker.
"Will you be my helper?" he asked.
Sneaker smiled back and said . . .

"YESSSSSS!"